Leo the Lightning Bug

by Eric Drachman
illustrated by James Muscarello

Kidwick
books

For the brave little lightning bug whose light shone
through the storm that night and inspired Leo's story.

Kidwick
books

Copyright © 2001 Eric Drachman

Voices on CD: Benjamin Drachman (Leo), Eric Drachman (Narrator, Lester),
Julia Drachman (Louise), Kati Garcia-Renart (Leo's Mom)
Music excerpts on CD from "Pairs of Pieces" courtesy of The Piatigorsky Foundation
Scherzo by Gregor Piatigorsky
The Swan by Camille Saint-Saëns
Evan Drachman, cello; Richard Dowling, piano

Illustrations were created with pastel and acrylic paint on colored matte board.

Text design and layout by Andrew Leman

Published in the United States
Printed in Korea
Distributed by National Book Network

Publisher's Cataloging-in-Publication
(Provided by Quality Books, Inc.)

Drachman, Eric.
  Leo the lightning bug / by Eric Drachman ;
illustrated by James Muscarello. -- 1st ed.
  p. cm.
  SUMMARY: Leo was the littlest lightning bug that he
knew. Not only was he little, he couldn't make a light
like all the other lightning bugs. Then one day, after
lots of practice, Leo finds the secret to making
light--and learns something about himself and the value
of self-confidence.
  Audience: Ages 4-7.
  LCCN 2001116806
  ISBN 10: 0-9703809-0-9
  ISBN 13: 978-0-9703809-0-6

  1. Fireflies--Juvenile fiction. 2. Self-confidence
in children--Juvenile fiction. [1. Fireflies--Fiction.
2. Self-confidence--Fiction.] I. Muscarello, James.
II. Title.

PZ7.D7797Le 2001   [E]
                QBI01-700355

Leo was a lightning bug.

He was a little lightning bug.

In fact, he was the littlest lightning bug of all
the lightning bugs he knew. He was littler than
Larry and Lester. He was even littler than Louise,
who wasn't a very big lightning bug herself.

"Leo. Leo! Even my name is small!" cried Leo.

"Oh no, Leo, not at all." explained his mother. "The name 'Leo' means 'Lion'. Inside, you're as big and brave as a lion!" and as she said this, her lightning bug light lit up brightly.

"But I can't even make a light, like Larry or Lester or even Louise!"

"You will, Darling. With a little time and practice, you'll light up with a lovely yellow lightning bug light."

Leo's mother kissed her little lion, turned on his nightlight, and closed his door — but not all the way, of course.

"I'm no lion," thought Leo, "but I guess I'll keep trying."

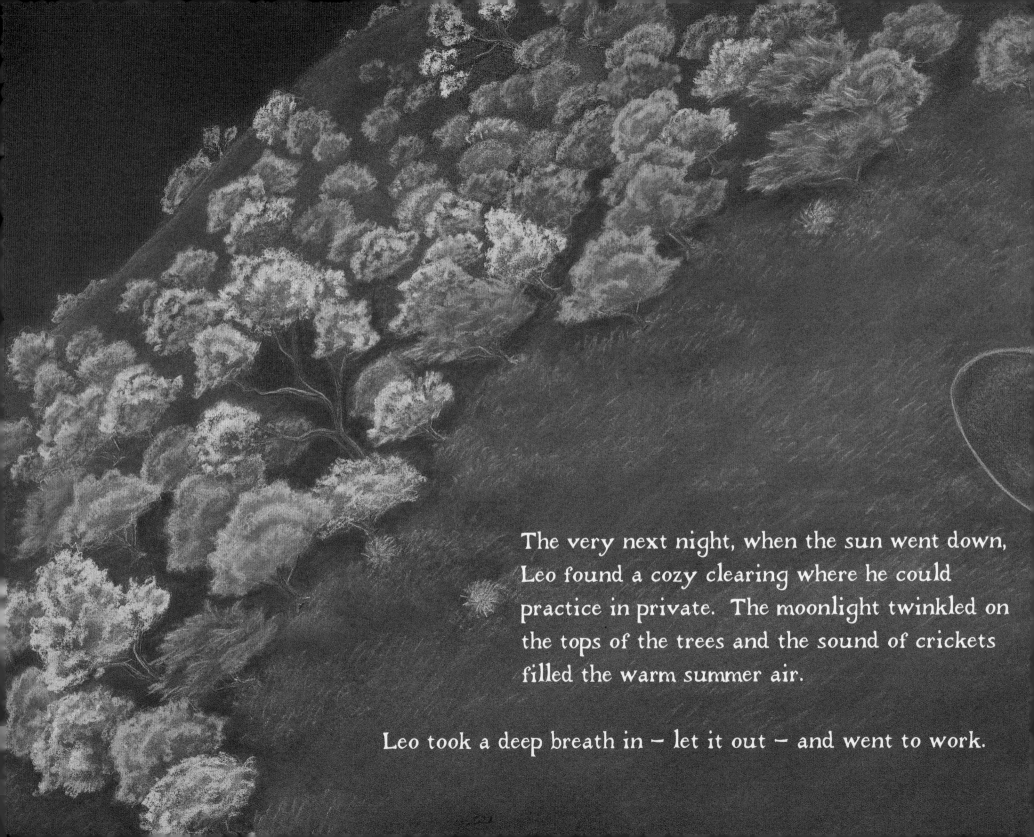

The very next night, when the sun went down, Leo found a cozy clearing where he could practice in private. The moonlight twinkled on the tops of the trees and the sound of crickets filled the warm summer air.

Leo took a deep breath in – let it out – and went to work.

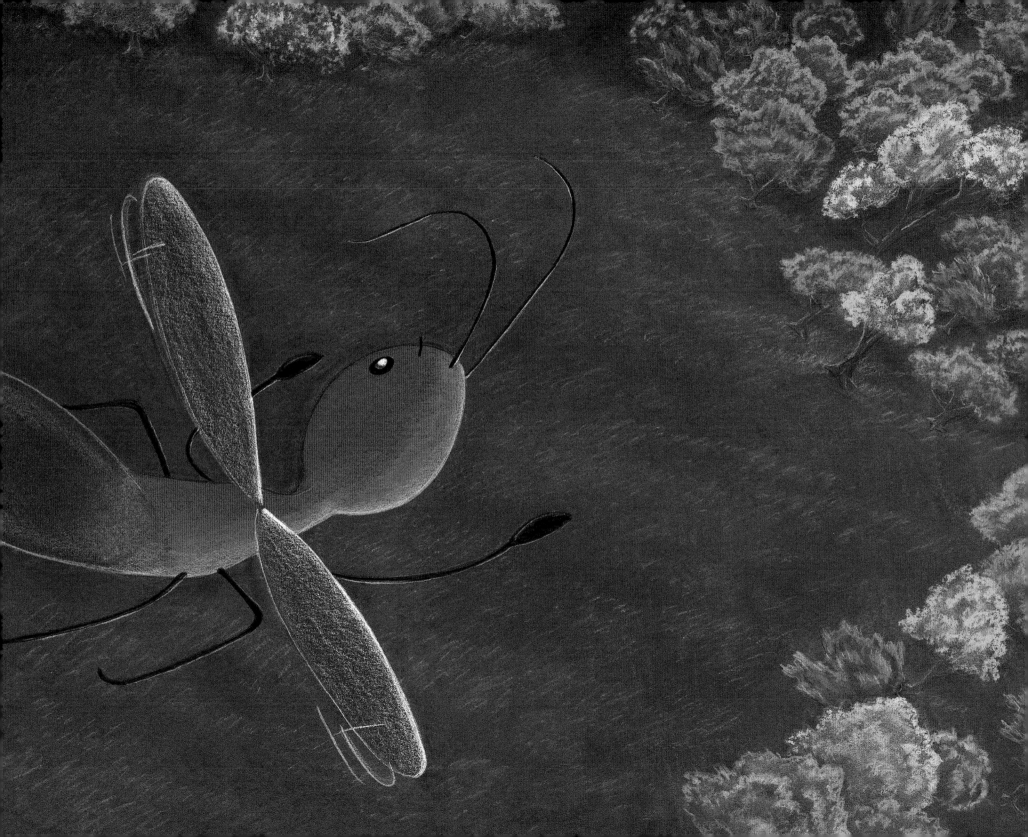

He started off with a little squeeze...

No light.

Then a push...

No light.

Then a big *oomph!*

...Still no light!

"Hmmm... Maybe with a running start," Leo thought... and he flew all the way back to the edge of the clearing. Meanwhile, Larry, Lester, and Louise had discovered Leo's not-so-private practice place. They ducked behind a twig to watch, and giggled at little Leo's efforts.

Leo had his head down and was flapping his wings as fast as
he could. When he reached his absolute top speed, he folded his
wings, lifted his feet, and slid on his rear end! He clenched all
of his toes on all six of his feet on all six of his legs, he
squinched his face and all of his muscles, and he squeeeeezed!

But looking down...

Leo found...

Nothing. Not even a glimmer.

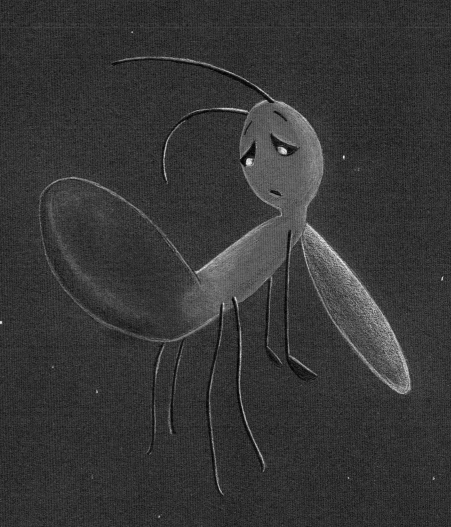

He did hear something though — Larry, Lester, and Louise
were out in the open now, laughing loudly at Leo's light...

...or rather — at his lack of a light.

Like almost all people and bugs and fish and animals of every kind,
Leo did not like to be laughed at. His knees felt weak, his face felt hot,
and he just wanted to *disappear!*

He flew and flew as fast as his wings
could go, until he finally found a very
dark cave where he could hide.

"Perfect," thought Leo, "a lightless
lightning bug deserves to be in the dark."
He sat there all alone and cried.

Then he cried some more.

When Leo was finished being sad, he got angry.
"I'll never make a light!! ...never make a light!! ...never make a light!!"
he yelled, and it echoed inside the cave.

Leo sat in silence, wondering what to do.

Then all of a sudden... the cave echoed.
   "With a little time time time...
   ...and practice practice practice..."

"Practice," remembered Leo. "That's what Mom
said! I have to practice. I have to practice, I have
to practice, I have to practice..." and he leapt up
and flew out of the cave.

Leo was so excited, he didn't even care about the storm now raging outside. As he got tossed by the wind and splashed by the rain, he kept squeezing and pushing and squinching, until finally...

CRAAACKKKKKK!!!!!

The entire sky lit up like daylight and there was a CRASH BOOM RIPPING sound! Leo felt his whole little body tremble with the noise.

The crickets stopped chirping and hid beneath the grass. Leo, who had never before even made a little lightning bug light, thought he had made that bright light and crashing sound.

It was a little scary, but he tried again...
and it was... fantastic! First, Leo's light
lit up — his very own light — and then
there was a bright flash in the sky and a
BIG... *BOOOOOM!!!!*

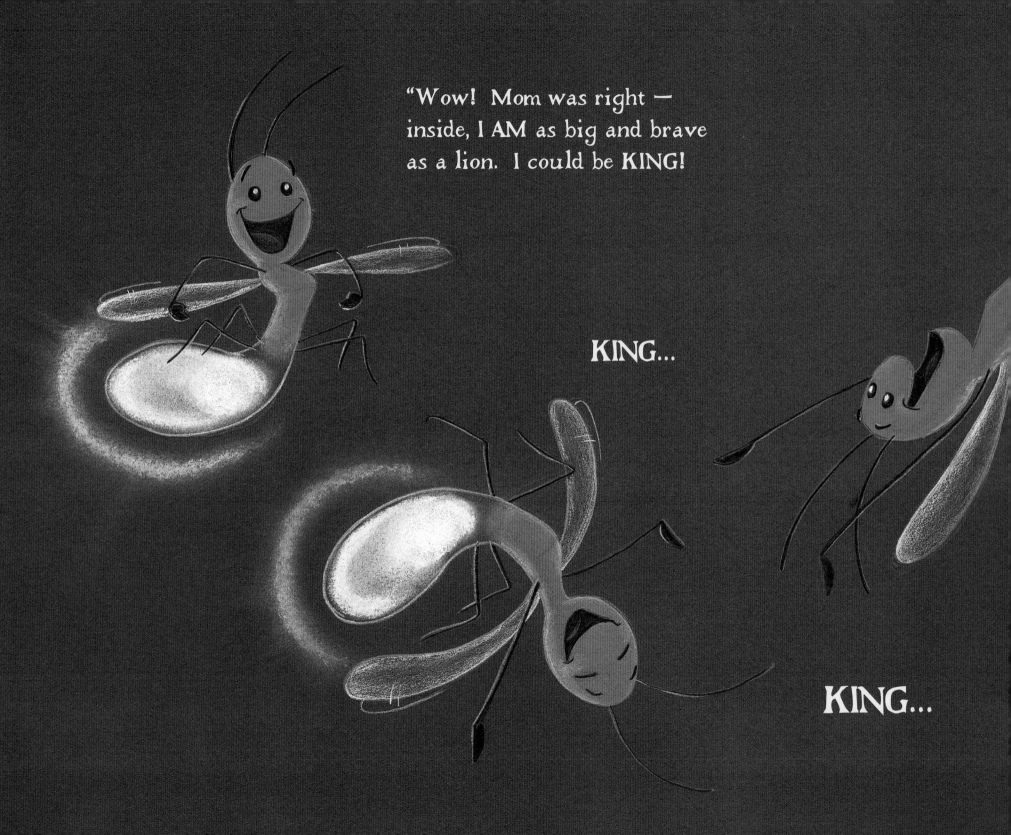

"Wow! Mom was right — inside, I AM as big and brave as a lion. I could be KING!

KING...

KING...

KING-OF-THE-LIGHTNING-BUGS!!!!"

And he danced a
KING-OF-THE-LIGHTNING-BUGS dance.

When the rain let up and the clouds cleared away, Leo
stopped laughing and dancing and headed for home.

Larry, Lester, and Louise were waiting for
Leo just outside his house.
"We saw you in the woods!" teased Louise,
and the three of them burst out laughing.

Just then, the strangest thing happened to Leo... or actually... DIDN'T happen... Leo did NOT feel angry... or embarrassed... or scared, or anything! He had a lion inside him.

"Yeah," Leo giggled, "I guess I did look pretty funny."

"Hey everybody! Look at me – I'm Leo!" yelled Lester, flapping his wings and running in circles. Suddenly, he tripped on one of his other feet and landed face first right smack in front of Leo himself.

When Lester looked up at Leo with a mouth full of dirt,
Leo laughed so hard that his whole body shook. Louise and
Larry were laughing too, and pretty soon... so was Lester.

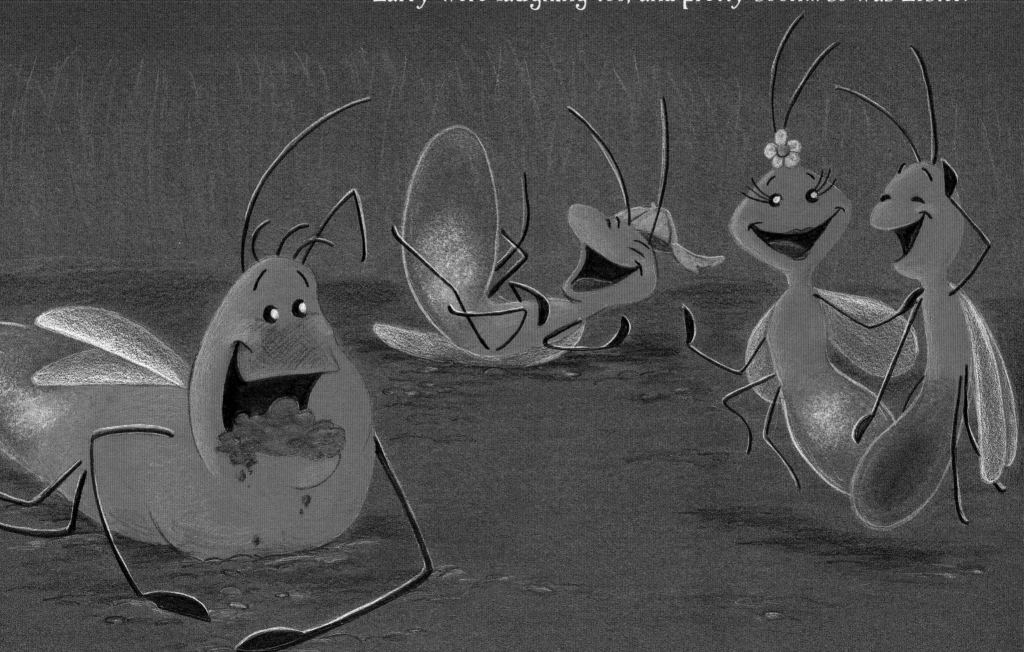

When they finally settled down, Leo said goodnight, and opened the door to his house.

"Leo!" coughed Lester. "Leo – you want to come play tomorrow?"

"I'd like that," he smiled, and his yellow light lit up in the night.

"Hey, Leo!" squealed Louise. "Look! Your light!"

"Yeah," Leo smiled proudly, "I know!" and he went into the house.

Later that night, when his mother came
to tuck him in, Leo was glowing...

...right through the covers.

She smiled to herself and gave him a kiss.
"I am so proud of you," she whispered.

And Leo said...

Nothing...

...for he was already fast asleep.